Magical
Mix-Ups

D1167519

Birthdays
and
Bridesmaids

First U.S. edition 2012

Library of Congress Cataloging-in-Publication Data is available.

Library of Congress Catalog Card Number pending

ISBN 978-0-7636-6272-1

12 13 14 15 16 17 BVG 10 9 8 7 6 5 4 3 2 1

Printed in Berryville, VA, U.S.A.

This book was typeset in Bell MT.
The illustrations were created digitally.

Nosy Crow
an imprint of
Candlewick Press
99 Dover Street
Somerville, Massachusetts 02144

www.nosycrow.com
www.candlewick.com

Magical Mix-Ups

Birthdays and Bridesmaids

Marnie Edwards * Leigh Hodgkinson

nosy crow

An imprint of Candlewick Press

Who's who in MIXTOPIA

Emerald the Witch

Princess Sapphire

Boris—Emerald's toad

Who's who in
FAIRYLAND

King
Tootsie

Twinkle

Queen
Mimsy

Prince
Peasebottom

Princess
Sneezebelle

You'll need these. . . .

Drawing
- - - - -
TOOLS

Using different tools helps
create great drawings.

PENCIL

COLORED PENCIL

CRAYON

Decorating TOOLS

Stick these in to add extra **SPARKLE** and **MAGIC**.

Sequins

Candy wrappers

Tinfoil

Glitter

Drawing Tips
Turn to the back of the book for drawing and design ideas!

GLitteR
READY
- - - - -

GET
SET

GO!

Chapter 1

WELCOME to Mixtopia!

Mixtopia is a magical land where you should expect the unexpected. A scruffy little witch named Emerald lives there with her trusty toad, Boris, and they think it's the best place in the world. . . .

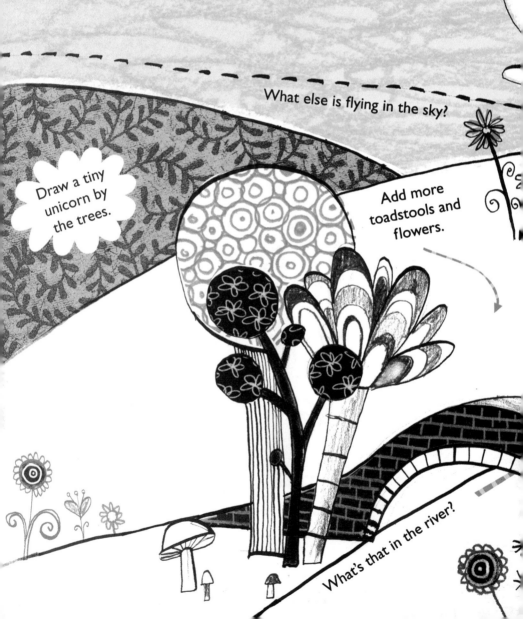

What else is flying in the sky?

Draw a tiny unicorn by the trees.

Add more toadstools and flowers.

What's that in the river?

Design your own patterns on the trees.

Flying overhead, Emerald spies the Royal Castle,
where her best friend, Princess Sapphire, lives.
Next door is a small cottage. Emerald sighs happily.
"Home, sweet home!"

Emerald puts her broomstick away neatly in the shed, then gives her caldron a stir.
"Hmm, needs more eye of newt, I think," she says, popping one in.

Is Emerald's house messy or clean?

Add more ingredients to the caldron.

A foul smell comes from the concoction, but Emerald doesn't mind. Suddenly she notices a big, fat envelope propped up on the table. . . .

What jars are on the shelves?

What's on the labels?

Draw a fancy stamp.

Draw Boris's long, curly tongue.

EMERALD

Emerald opens the envelope, and her hair sparks with excitement. Inside is a very fancy invitation. "Quick, Boris, let's show Sapphire," says Emerald.

Draw lots of warts on Boris.

Decorate the invitation.

Dear Emerald the Witch

King Tootsie and Queen Mimsy
of Fairyland
would love you to come to the
wedding of their daughter

Princess Sneezebelle
to
Prince Peasebottom

Wednesday at 2 p.m.
Please, please come!

And bring your dancing shoes!

Emerald and Boris crash through Princess Sapphire's open bedroom window.

"Now look what you've done, Em!" cries Sapphire, practically jumping out of her lovely skin. "I've smudged my nails."

"Never mind that,"
says Emerald. "Look!"
"Snap!" cries Sapphire. "I'm so excited.
I just can't decide what to wear. . . ."

What face is Boris making?

Fill in the envelopes.

Are there lots of toys on the bed?

Look at all the clothes on the floor!

Add to the tiara tree.

Chapter 2

What
<u>NOT</u> to
Wear

What else is in the closet?

Princess Sapphire is trying on dresses. "What do you think, Em?" she asks.

What is Sapphire wearing?

Decorate the dresses with pretty patterns.

"Should I have my hair up or down?" asks Sapphire.

Give Sapphire a lovely hairstyle and a tiara.

Is Emerald looking bored or fascinated?

Accessorize Sapphire with rings, bracelets, and a necklace.

"Shoes!" Sapphire turns to look at her vast collection. "Which go best?"

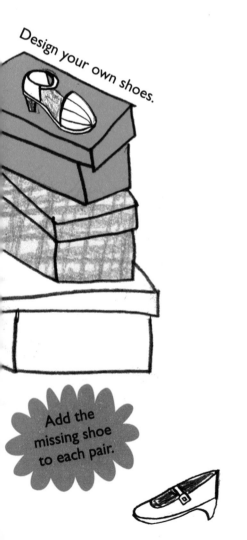

Design your own shoes.

Add the missing shoe to each pair.

"Oh, wake up, Em!" cries Sapphire, catching her friend snoozing. "What are *you* going to wear, anyway? Not that old thing.

Or anything black.

I know. . . ."

What does Boris think of Emerald's new look?

Soon Emerald has had enough. With a wave
of her wand, she magics up an outfit she likes.
Princess Sapphire looks on in approval.

What does her
witchy outfit look like?
Is it right for the
royal wedding?

"Our carriage leaves first thing tomorrow,"
Sapphire tells her friend. "And just one thing:
that horrible toad stays at home!"

Draw some
smelly sniff
lines around
Boris.

Add a swirly
pattern to
Boris's dress.

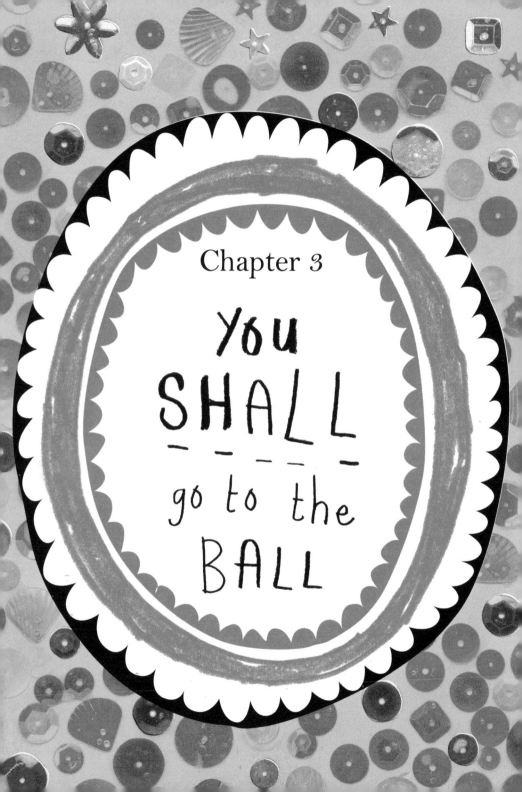

Chapter 3

You
SHALL
- - - - -
go to the
BALL

The two girls set off for Fairyland in a beautiful unicorn-drawn carriage.

Princess Sapphire's many bags are strapped to its roof, and a footman is holding her hatboxes . . . and the carriage reins!

Add the reins and more tiny unicorns.

The carriage goes over a bump, and Princess Sapphire yelps, rubbing her royal bottom.
"Oh! It's worse than that time I slept on a pea! I'll be black and blue—hey . . . !"

What a lovely view!

What's in this pocket?

She points an accusing finger at Emerald's cloak. "Something moved. . . ."

Is it rainy or sunny?

What toys and games are on the floor?

It's Boris!

"I couldn't leave him. He'd have been so lonely, Sapphy," explains Emerald.

Draw drool on Boris.

What's in the picnic basket?

Put some Boris treats here.

"Just make sure he doesn't eat a fairy, then," mutters her friend darkly.

Boris tries not to drool.

What is Sapphire about to eat?

Finish this pillar.

Draw the Magic Gates.

Just then, they hear the tinkling of bells. As they go through the tiny Magic Gates into Fairyland, they feel themselves shrinking. "We're fairy-size!" cries Sapphire

Fill in their passport details.

BUTTERFLY
ISLAND
APRIL 15, 2010

JANUARY 29
WITCH
WORLD
2011

Name:

Address:

Age:

Occupation:

Add more travel stamps

Name:

Address:

Age:

Occupation:

MERMAIDIA
OCTOBER
25TH
2009

Who's standing guard?

What do Sapphire and Emerald's passport photos look like?

The now-tiny carriage sweeps up the
driveway to the amazing Fairy Palace.

They've arrived!

buzz buzz

Decorate
the wings,
and add more
butterflies.

Finish decorating the Palace.

Add spots.

Draw more flowers.

A lovely fairy flutters down
the steps to greet them.

Add wings
to the fairy
footmen.

What is this fairy
footman carrying?

"Darlings!"
cries Queen Mimsy.
"You're just in time
for tea!"

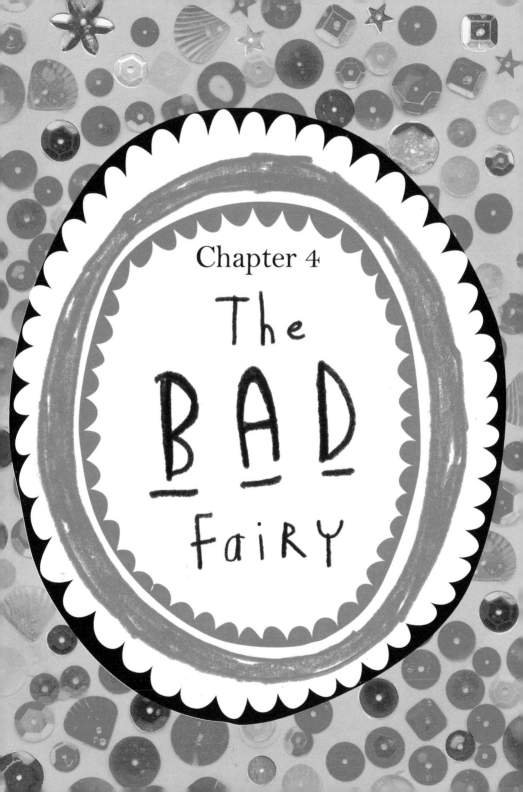

Chapter 4

The
BAD
FaiRY

Finish the fairy throne.

Just as Emerald is reaching for her fifth cucumber sandwich, the door to the Throne Room crashes open.

Add some yummy cupcakes!

Draw in the fairy tea set.

Princess Sneezebelle rushes in, holding a velvet ring box and waving a piece of paper around.

"The Fairy Rings!
    They've been **stolen!**" she cries.

The paper falls to the floor.
The thief has left a note!

HA HA HA HA HA!

NO rings means

NO wedding

SERVES YOU RIGHT for spoiling EVERYTHING!

signed

The note is from Twinkle. Write her name here. →

Princess Sneezebelle sniffs and holds out
the ring box. "Look what she left instead!"
Two Squirt Rings nestle against the soft velvet.
"Who's Twinkle?" asks Emerald.
  "She's Sneezebelle's little cousin,"
    explains Queen Mimsy.

"We have to find her and get the rings back, or the wedding is off!"

At this, Princess Sneezebelle faints delicately onto the chaise longue.

Emerald and Sapphire go to their room to unpack.
Downstairs, all is fairy chaos.

"Why don't we try to find Twinkle?" says Emerald.
"Maybe the Squirt Rings are a clue."

Add some flowers.

Draw a lampshade.

Where is Boris?

What's on the floor?

They decide to go to Main Street
to see if they can find a shop that sells
Squirt Rings.

Someone might remember Twinkle!

WANDS 'R' US

Finish the
shop fronts.

What's flying by?

Who's in the windows?

TOADSTOOLZ

Add some fairy pets.

A shop called Parties for Smarties is having a sale:
"Buy 2 Squirt Rings, get a Wiggle Snake free!"

"Look!" cries Princess Sapphire, pointing.
"I bet that's where Twinkle got
her rings."

ONLY
2
SCHOOL
FAIRIES
ALLOWED
IN SHOP AT
ONE TIME

Who
else is going
shopping?

Design a colorful poster advertising party goodies.

Chapter 5

HOT
on the
TRAIL!

WIGGLE WORMS

MAGIC BUBBLE WANDS

Add funny wigs here.

Fill up the boxes.

GLITTER PENS

GLOW IN THE DARK BOUNCY BALLS

MONSTER PENCIL TOPPERS

The Party Fairy is very helpful.
"Twinkle was here yesterday," he explains. "She said she'd been saving up all her pocket money, and she spent quite a lot of it on Squirt Rings, party bags, and helium balloons. Then she went off to the bakery!"

Fill up all the shelves in the shop.

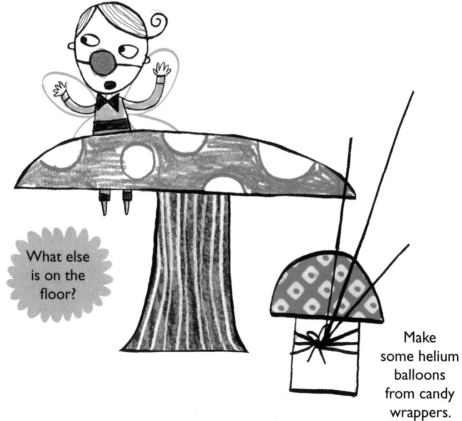

What else is on the floor?

Make some helium balloons from candy wrappers.

The two girls thank the Party Fairy and head for the bakery. "Hmmm," says Sapphire. "Squirt Rings, party bags, and balloons—what could it all mean?" "Maybe there'll be more clues at the bakery?" suggests Emerald.

Draw the schoolgirl fairies lining up at the door.

What's Boris looking at through his magnifying glass?

What notes has Boris made?

Finish Boris's dotted line.

The bakery is heavenly. There are tiny little cupcakes and enormous chocolate cakes. The meringues look light and fluffy, and as for the cream puffs . . . !

Finish these cupcakes.

Draw a delicious cake in here.

The Fairy Baker is putting the finishing touches on an enormous wedding cake and looks a bit frazzled. "May I help you?" she asks.

The friends ask about Twinkle,
and the fairy points at a large cake box on
the counter. "She'll be here in a minute,"
she says, "to pick up her cupcakes."

What do
the cakes
spell?

Inside the box are twenty beautiful little cupcakes,
all decorated with sprinkles, glitter, and letters. . . .

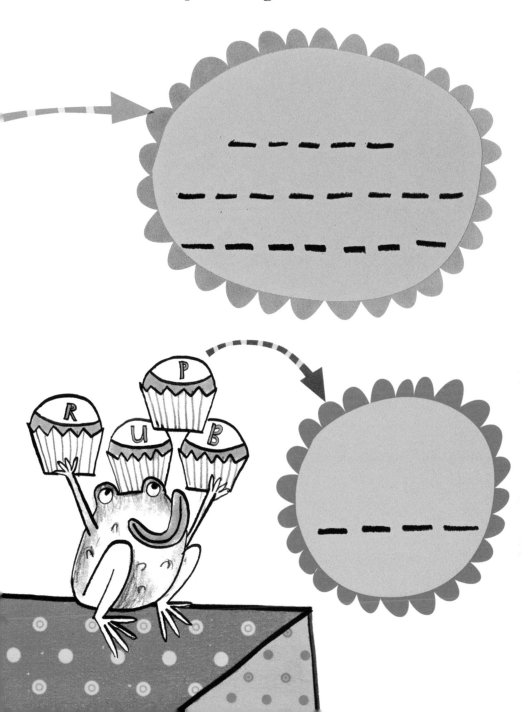

Fairy Bakery Menu

Design your own wallpaper for the bakery walls.

Emerald and Sapphire sit down to wait
for Twinkle. They order hot chocolate
and dainty cookies, and Sapphire
puts on a pair of huge sunglasses.
"I'm in disguise!" she says.
Emerald sighs and takes off her hat.
"I can't help thinking those cupcakes
were a clue. . . ."

Suddenly the shop doorbell tinkles and makes them all jump. Boris falls off Emerald's head into a jar of whipped cream.

Who is coming through the door?

What has the Fairy Baker dropped?

Add more splashes.

Decorate the label.

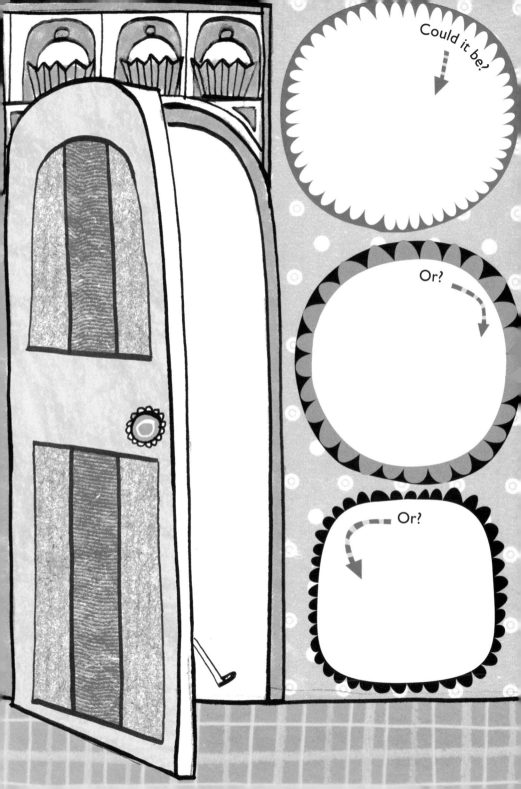

It's Twinkle!
And look what she's wearing around her neck!

Draw a big gloom cloud over Twinkle.

Add a pattern to the floor.

Chapter 6

WEDDING

Belles

Finish designing the awning.

Fairy Bakery

Twinkle puts her box of cupcakes in her bike basket. "Excuse me," says Sapphire, "but are those the Royal Wedding Rings?"

Attach Twinkle's helium balloons to her bike handle.

Add Twinkle's cupcakes and party things.

"It's my birthday tomorrow, but everyone's forgotten because of the PESKY Royal Wedding!" exclaims Twinkle. "I thought if I took the rings, it would stop the wedding and everyone would come to my party instead. I'm really sorry. . . ."

Add a pile of birthday presents.

"Let's go and talk to the Queen," says Emerald, waving her wand. They arrive at the Palace in a puff of smoke, causing some fairy alarm. But Twinkle is soon forgiven.

Finish the magic-wand swirl.

Add more stars.

Then Queen Mimsy has a great idea.
"Let's have a magical mix-up: a fantastic
wedding and birthday party in one!"

Finish the fairy faces.

Draw an idea lightbulb above Queen Mimsy.

"I can't wait to see Princess Sneezebelle's dress!" says Sapphire the next day as she waits impatiently for the bride to arrive at the Fairy Bower.

"And Twinkle's!" says Emerald.
"Here they come!"

Add a perfect rainbow here.

Where is Boris?

Add fancy hats to the fairy guests.

Draw the Elf King.

Draw some magical creatures here.

After the ceremony, they all go back to the Palace for a really royal wedding-birthday feast!

Add more love hearts.

Boris is the wedding photographer. Give him a camera.

Finish the wedding-cake decorations.

Finish the tablecloth pattern.

As night falls and the stars come out, the Fairy
Dance starts. Soon Fairyland is really rocking!

Give the Fairy
DJ headphones.

Who is
this crazy
dancer?

After the celebration, Emerald and
Sapphire travel back to Mixtopia.
"What a fantastic wedding-birthday!"
says Sapphire.

Decorate their
goodie bags.

What's in
Sapphire's
goodie bag?

Emerald agrees. "And Twinkle's are the best goodie bags ever!"

What great photos Boris took!

The Big Picture

Draw your favorite moments from the book, and add some decorative tidbits.

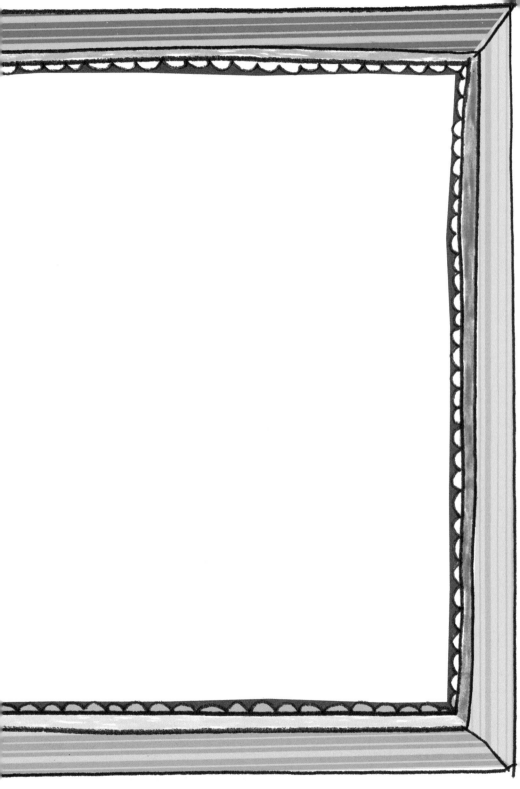

picture
GLOSSARY

If you need a helping hand thinking of things to draw, then check these ideas out!

cuddly toys

schoolgirl fairy

Boris's treats

FLY JAM

SNAIL JUICE

stars

dresses